Josue

Pirates Don't Wear Pink Sunglasses

D0096698

by Debbie Dadey
and
Marcia Thornton Jones

illustrated by John Steven Gurney

A
LITTLE APPLE
PAPERBACK

SCHOLASTIC INC.
New York   Toronto   London   Auckland   Sydney

To
Ruth and Charles Dadey
and
Charlene and Walter Jones

No part of this publication may be reproduced in whole or in part, or stored in a retrieval system, or transmitted in any form or by any means, electronic, mechanical, photocopying, recording, or otherwise, without written permission of the publisher. For information regarding permission, write to Scholastic Inc., 555 Broadway, New York, New York 10012.

ISBN 0-590-47298-4

Copyright © 1994 by Marcia Thornton Jones and Debbie S. Dadey. All rights reserved. Published by Scholastic Inc. APPLE PAPERBACKS is a registered trademark of Scholastic Inc.

36 35 34 33 32 31 .   3/0

Printed in the U.S.A.   40

First Scholastic printing, May 1994

Book design by Laurie McBarnette

1

Mistletoe

"I can't believe we have to go back there," Melody complained as the school bus went over a bump.

Liza leaned her head out the bus window and moaned, "We'll never make it out of there alive. Mr. Jenkins will get us for sure this time."

The Bailey Elementary kids nodded as they remembered last summer at Camp Lone Wolf. They were sure Mr. Jenkins, their camp counselor, was a werewolf.

"He'll have to deal with me first," Eddie said from the seat behind the two girls. He held up a large clump of mistletoe.

"All right!" Howie slapped his friend Eddie on the back. "That should keep old werewolf-face in check." The kids had read in a book that people during the

Middle Ages used mistletoe to scare away werewolves.

Eddie stuffed the mistletoe into his blue Bailey City gym bag. "I still don't believe Mr. Jenkins is really a werewolf, but just in case. . . ."

"You're ready," Melody finished for him.

The four kids were silent as the bus passed the sign that said *Welcome to Camp Lone Wolf*. Tall weeds clung to the weathered sign. As the bus bumped over the gravel drive, Coach Ellison stood up in the front of the bus and grinned at the Bailey School kids.

"I always look forward to this nature trip," he said, rubbing his hands together. "Especially the boat race on Friday against the Sheldon Sharks."

"I don't know why," Liza mumbled. "Bailey School NEVER wins."

Melody nodded. "All we end up with are mosquito bites."

Every year the kids from Bailey Elementary went on a week-long nature trip. And every year the field trip ended with a rowing competition against the kids from nearby Sheldon City. The Bailey Boaters had never won a single race.

"But this time Coach Ellison says we're going to have a professional instructor," Howie told her.

"If Mr. Jenkins doesn't get us first." Melody shivered as she remembered Mr.

Jenkins' wolf-like howls.

"Maybe Mr. Jenkins won't even be there," Liza said.

"Yeah, maybe he retired to the Old Werewolves' Home," Melody said hopefully.

Eddie shook his curly red head and pointed. "Not a chance. Look!"

As the bus squeaked to a stop, the four kids saw a very hairy Mr. Jenkins standing beside a picnic table. He wore no shoes, a brown Camp Lone Wolf T-shirt, and ragged blue jeans. Around his furry neck were silver dog tags. Beside him stood a stocky man with a long black beard and bright pink sunglasses. The stranger's frizzy black hair was tied back in a ponytail with a purple bandana, and a silver earring dangled from his left ear.

"Oh, no!" Melody gasped. "Now there's two of them!"

Howie gulped. "It's a werewolf convention."

"Everybody off!" Coach Ellison hollered from the front of the bus. "Let's get ready for those Sheldon Sharks!"

Liza followed her friends off the bus. "I just hope we don't get eaten first!"

2

Captain Teach

"Welcome to Camp Lone Wolf, Bailey kids," Mr. Jenkins boomed in a voice loud enough to rattle the bus windows. "I hope you're ready to work those rowing muscles of yours."

"I hope he doesn't make a snack out of my muscles," Melody whispered, but she quickly fell silent when Mr. Jenkins glared at her. His eyes were bloodshot and underlined with dark circles. He looked like he hadn't slept since the last time she'd seen him.

"It's kind of you to give us a discount," Coach Ellison said. "The school couldn't afford to pay full price."

Mr. Jenkins scratched his tangled beard and shrugged. "Business has been slow. At least this way the camp is earning some money. And I was lucky to run into Captain Teach. He's helping out at no cost." Mr. Jenkins nodded to the burly man. "Teach knows all about making a crew shipshape, so you rookies pay attention and you'll win that boat race."

"I'd rather eat hot dogs and ice cream," Eddie laughed. But his smile faded when Mr. Jenkins grinned back, showing all his teeth.

Mr. Jenkins licked his lips. "We'll worry about eating later, after Teach is through with you."

Liza gulped. "I'm already worried."

"They're all yours," Mr. Jenkins told Captain Teach as he stalked into the woods.

Coach Ellison held his hand out to the new instructor. "Hello, I'm Frank Ellison, the Bailey coach." Instead of shaking his hand, Captain Teach spit on the dusty ground and adjusted his pink sunglasses.

Coach Ellison dropped his hand to his side and stammered, "We're honored to have an experienced instructor. Where did you get your experience?"

Captain Teach scowled and spoke with a gruff accent. "Me life has been the sea, and I work where the tide takes me." He winked at Coach Ellison and then turned to the kids clustered by the bus. "Why are you sailors loafing about?" he growled. "Get your gear stowed in the cabins and then hightail it to the docks. We've work to do."

The kids ran into each other as they grabbed their bags and headed for the cabins.

Melody, Liza, and the other girls dumped their bags on the bunks in Cabin Gray Wolf. Dust clouds poofed from the mattresses and made them sneeze. "This place is filthy," Melody snapped. "It looks like no one has been here since we left."

Liza knocked some cobwebs down with a pillow. "You're probably right. Everybody's started going to Camp Soaring Eagle on the other side of Sheldon City."

"Camp Soaring Eagle is fantastic," Carey said. "It's much better than this flea nest. It has horses, motor scooters, and even scuba gear. I went there for two weeks! It was a blast!" Carey's father was the president of the Bailey City bank, and she always got to do whatever she

wanted. Most of the kids thought she was a brat.

"I don't think Camp Lone Wolf can afford that stuff," Liza said.

"It won't be able to afford to stay open if it doesn't do something fast," Carey snapped. "My dad said this place is broke. If they don't make this month's payment, Bailey Bank is going to take over."

"What does a bank want with a camp?" Melody asked.

Carey smiled. "They're going to sell it to Mega-Mall Development Company so Bailey City can have the biggest mall in the country."

"But we already have a mall," Melody reminded Carey.

Liza looked out the dusty window at all of the tall pine trees. "It'd be a shame to tear down all those trees. And what about the animals and Mr. Jenkins?"

Carey shrugged. "Who cares about that

mangy man and all those nasty creatures? A mall would be great!"

"I'm not so sure," Liza muttered as the girls headed back outside.

They met Eddie and Howie outside Cabin Silver Wolf. Tall weeds sprouted around the cabin. "This place is a mess," Howie said.

"It's gone to the dogs," Eddie laughed. "Or should I say the wolves?"

Liza's face turned pale. "Maybe wolves have taken over. After all, I haven't seen any other camp counselors."

"Liza's right," Melody said.

Eddie laughed at his friends. "I have plenty of mistletoe with me. Besides, Coach Ellison and Captain Teach are here. We have nothing to worry about."

Howie took a deep breath and looked at his friend. "I hope you're right."

3

Long-Tongued Jack

Coach Ellison herded the group down to the lake where Captain Teach waited. He stood on two boats, with one foot in each boat.

Melody nodded. "Look at his parrot." Perched on Teach's shoulder was a large yellow-and-green bird with a bright orange beak.

"Morning," the bird chirped.

"Oh, how sweet," Carey said.

"Row, mate!" the bird squawked.

Eddie laughed. "Sweet, just like poison."

"Hardee, har, har," Captain Teach laughed and pushed up his sunglasses. "Long-Tongued Jack here says it be time to get started. We've no time to waste if you're going to win that race."

"But we can't win," Liza whined. "The Sheldon City Sharks always beat the Bailey Boaters."

"Can't never wins! Can't never wins!" Long-Tongued Jack squawked and raised his colorful wings.

"Jack's right," Teach roared. "We'll have no lily-livered quitters here. Captain Teach never gives up without a fight."

"Even if we're the worst rowers in the state?" Eddie asked.

"Especially then," Teach said and adjusted his pink sunglasses. "We'll catch those Sheldon big shots off guard. They'll never know what hit them."

"Now you're talking." Eddie smiled, but the rest of the kids still looked uncertain.

"Surely you pint-sized pieces of fish bait know the story of Molly the Red?" Captain Teach looked at the kids shaking their heads.

"Molly the Red, Molly the Red!" Long-Tongued Jack screeched and flew over to Coach Ellison and sat on his head. A few kids snickered. Coach Ellison stood very still as Teach began telling his story.

"It was back in 1718 when pirates still ruled the seas. Molly the Red was the fiercest pirate ever to sail up the Northern Coast. Most pirates were content to stay near the Barbary Coast where it was safe. But not Molly. She feared not a thing, 'cepting maybe Blackbeard himself."

A few kids nodded their heads in recognition of the name Blackbeard, the most famous pirate who ever lived.

"Molly's ship was loaded with riches she'd looted from ships sailing from the East Coast harbors. She needed a place to hide out for a while to bury her treasures. That place was —"

"Bailey City," Coach Ellison interrupted.

Long-Tongued Jack flapped his wings and squawked, "Bailey Treasure! Bailey Treasure!"

"But Bailey City isn't on the ocean," Howie pointed out.

"Aye. A smart lad you be. The original settlement of Bailey City was right here on the shores of the Red River, which flows into the Atlantic."

"I never knew pirates were in Bailey City," Liza said with wide eyes.

Teach shook his head. "The scallywags never made it. Molly thought that Bailey City would be an easy mark of yellow-bellied men and women, a good place to rob and plunder and hide out. But Bailey City had a surprise for her."

"What happened?" Melody asked.

"When some of the gentle folk of Bailey City heard that Molly's thieving rascals were on their way, they ran off. But some had the guts to stay. They built barricades and practiced with their weapons, women and men alike. They were ready when Molly's ship, heavy with treasure, rounded the bend to Bailey City."

"Did Molly's pirates loot Bailey City?" Howie asked.

"Hardee, har, har," Captain Teach roared. "Hardly! The men and women of Bailey City blew that ship clear out of the water."

"What about the treasure?" Carey asked.

"Never found," Teach whispered. "Some think it's still here, buried by that thieving woman somewhere on the shores of the Red River."

The kids looked at the blue water, wondering about the treasure, until Eddie interrupted. "This is all very interesting," he said to Captain Teach, "but what does it have to do with the race?"

"Everything!" Teach said, slowly adjusting his pink sunglasses. "We're going to do the same thing to the Sheldon Sharks that they did to Molly the Red. We're going to blow them out of the water!"

4

Treasure

"You scallywags look to be getting the hang of it now, I see," Captain Teach bellowed from the dock. "Tomorrow you'll be ready for a real workout!"

"But we are working," Liza said. The entire third grade practiced rowing all afternoon under Captain Teach's strict command. Eddie started off by splashing the kids with his oars. But one "Buckle down, mate," from Captain Teach stopped Eddie's mischief.

"Watch out!" Liza screamed. Just as the four friends were getting the hang of rowing, a speed boat zipped past leaving huge waves in its wake. Eddie and Melody frantically turned the boat away from the rushing water while the waves crashed against their tiny boat. Howie

dropped his oar and Liza screamed.

"Hardee, har, har," Teach roared from the dock. "I see you landlubbers know nothing about water. If you see ripples coming at you, face them head-on. That way the waves will rock you like a baby in a cradle!"

After that, no one goofed off, and everyone improved. The next time a boat sped past, they rode out the waves like experts. "We're getting pretty good at this," Eddie bragged.

Captain Teach threw his head back and laughed. "You city slickers are barely moving the boat. You have a long way to go before you'll beat those Sheldon rogues."

"Sheldon rogues! Sheldon rogues!" Long-Tongued Jack screeched from Teach's shoulder. He flapped his wings when Captain Teach hopped into a boat. Teach showed Howie how to tie the boat to the dock with a tight hitching knot, then he grinned at the tired campers. "You rascals need to eat. You'll need to muster all your strength for tomorrow's workout," he said. "So eat hardy, mates!"

"All right, I'm starving," Liza cheered.

Captain Teach waited until the last boater was safely on the dock before he stomped off toward the cabins. The other boaters ran ahead with Coach Ellison, but Liza was too tired to keep up. Melody, Howie, and Eddie slowed down to walk with her.

"My arms are killing me," Liza said as the kids followed a good distance behind Captain Teach.

Melody nodded her head. "I've never worked so hard in my whole life."

"That Teach is a real battle-ax," Eddie agreed, looking up the trail at Teach's huge back, "but he might just make winners out of us."

"You mean you like him?" Howie asked, rubbing his sore arms.

Eddie shrugged. "I wouldn't exactly say I like him, but I do like to win. Captain Teach sure seems to know about rowing. If we keep this up, those Sheldon Sharks won't stand a chance. I never thought I'd say this, but I'm glad nature week is at Camp Lone Wolf."

"You better enjoy it here while you can," Liza told him. "Carey told us that the camp is probably going to close."

"What are you talking about?" Howie asked.

Melody explained, "The camp is losing money. If Mr. Jenkins can't make this month's payment, the bank is going to turn it into a huge mall."

Liza looked at the tree-lined trail and sighed. "I still think it would be a shame to tear down these huge old trees. I bet some of them were here when Molly the Red terrorized the first Bailey City."

"That's what Camp Lone Wolf needs," Howie told them. "Molly the Red's treasure."

"You're right," Melody agreed. "Captain Teach said it was never found."

"Maybe we could find it!" Liza squealed.

Eddie shook his head. "If it hasn't been found in over two hundred years, there's no way we could find it. We'd better concentrate on beating the Sheldon Sharks."

"I guess you're right," Liza said. "Still, it would be nice to save those big trees."

Eddie bent down to pick up a small green case that was in the middle of the trail. "I think Teach dropped this," he said.

"It's his sunglasses case," Liza said. "We can give it to him in the dining hall."

"It's empty except for a piece of paper,"

Eddie told his friends as he unsnapped the case.

"That's none of your business," Liza told him and tried to jerk the case away.

"Liza's right," Howie agreed.

"A little peek won't hurt anything," Eddie muttered. "Besides, we don't even know for sure it's Teach's. I'll see if there's a name inside." Eddie pulled a yellowed piece of paper from the back of the case and carefully unfolded it. Strange lines covered the small paper, and wispy handwriting filled one corner.

"There's a note on it," Eddie said.

Melody snatched the paper from

Eddie. "Reading other people's mail is against the law."

Eddie shrugged. "It's just an old map anyway."

"Why would Teach keep an old map in his sunglasses case?" Liza asked.

"He probably uses it to plan our rowing training," Howie suggested.

"Maybe we should keep it so he won't be able to plan any more killer workouts," Melody said as she folded the map and stuffed it back in the case.

"That wouldn't be honest," Liza told them. "We'll give it to him at dinner."

When they finally reached the dining hall, Coach Ellison was helping Mr. Jenkins grill hamburgers and hot dogs. But Captain Teach was nowhere in sight.

5

Blackbeard

"We have to give his sunglasses case to him," Liza told her friends. "He might be worried about it." The kids had swallowed down their entire supper of hot dogs, hamburgers, French fries, baked beans, and ice cream and still there was no sign of Captain Teach in the dining hall.

"We have plenty of time before the campfire," Melody said.

Eddie frowned and licked the last bit of ice cream off his fingers. "We don't know where Teach is staying."

"Teach is in that small cabin close to the boat dock," Carey said as she walked past their table to put up her food tray. "I saw him going there after he practically killed us this afternoon."

"It's settled then," Liza said, gathering up her tray. "We'll go right now."

"I don't know how I ever got mixed up with a bunch of turkeys like you guys," Eddie complained as they walked down the path to the lake.

"There's the cabin," Howie said. "I never even noticed it before." Howie pointed through the trees at a small cabin set back from the path. The gray wooden cabin had a tiny porch with a flag hanging from it.

"That's a weird flag," Melody said as they walked onto Captain Teach's porch. The flag was black with a white skull painted on it, and crossed bones were underneath the skull.

"That's a Jolly Roger," Howie told them. "Teach must like to study about pirates."

"How do you know that's a pirate flag?" Eddie asked, "For all you know, it could be the flag of Brazil. Maybe Teach is from Brazil."

"If you'd read a book once in a while you'd learn something," Howie said as he knocked on the door.

"He's not here," Eddie said. "Are you happy now? We walked all the way down here for nothing."

"Try one more time," Liza suggested.

Howie knocked on the door again. This time his pounding caused the door to slowly creak open. Howie peeked inside the cabin. He looked back at his friends and gulped. "Captain Teach isn't here, but you'll never believe what is."

Eddie pushed past Howie into the cabin. "Wow, this is neat!" Eddie shouted. The walls of the cabin were covered with swords, old guns, and yellow maps. A large bird perch stood near the window, and a bookcase was crammed full of model ships in glass bottles.

"I've always wanted one of these," Eddie said, picking up a huge ship in a bottle labeled *Queen Anne's Revenge*.

"You'd better put that down before you break it," Liza said. "We can just leave the case on the porch."

"I don't think we'd better leave anything," Howie told them. "I have a strange feeling about all this."

"What are you talking about?" Melody asked.

"Let me see that map again," Howie asked Melody. She shrugged and handed over the green case. Howie carefully unfolded the old map and held it up by the window to read its strange handwriting.

"You shouldn't read that," Liza reminded him.

Howie looked at Liza and spoke very seriously. "This may be a matter of life and death. Besides, this isn't a letter. It's just a note scribbled on a map."

"I guess it's okay. Can you read what it says?" Liza said.

Howie carefully smoothed out the old crinkled paper and tried to make out the words. He read, " 'My dearest Black-beard, I am doomed. I leave you my treasure and my love.' "

Liza squinted to read the strange hand-writing. "Do you think it's from Molly?"

"Molly the Red?" Melody asked.

Howie nodded his head. "And I bet this is a map telling Blackbeard where her treasure is buried."

"You're crazy," Eddie said, grabbing the map back. "What would Teach be doing with a pirate's map?"

"In the same book that had the pirate's flag, there was also a section about Black-beard," Howie told them.

"That makes sense," Melody said. She touched a huge sword that hung from the wall. "After all, Blackbeard was the most famous pirate who ever lived."

"Also the meanest," Eddie agreed.

Howie pointed to the ship in the bottle Eddie had held up. "That was his ship.

Read the name on the bottom of the label."

Eddie held the bottle up to read the label in the fading light. " '*Queen Anne's Revenge.* Ship of Blackbeard, Captain Edward Teach, killed 1718.' "

"Captain Teach!" Melody squealed.

"So what?" Eddie put the bottle back on the shelf. "You said yourself Teach likes to study about pirates. Captain Teach is probably his nickname."

Howie shook his head. "I don't think Teach just likes to study about pirates. I think he *is* a pirate."

Eddie laughed out loud. "Pirates lived a long time ago. There aren't any left today."

"Besides, who ever heard of a pirate wearing pink sunglasses?" Melody said.

"I don't know," Liza said. "Let's just leave the case and go."

"We can't." Howie shook his head. "We know too much. If this is a treasure map and Teach really is a pirate, we may be in a lot of danger."

"Danger. Danger. Squawk!"

The four kids jumped at the loud screech. There, perched on the window-sill, was Long-Tongued Jack.

6

Birdbrain

"Run!" Melody screamed and darted for the door along with her friends. They collided before they could squeeze through, and Liza went sprawling across the floor. Howie tripped over her and landed with a thump.

"Ouch!" Liza cried. "You hurt my leg."

"Peg leg! Peg leg!" Long-Tongued Jack crowed.

"I'd like to give you a peg leg, you birdbrain!" Eddie hissed at the bird.

Long-Tongued Jack flapped across the room and landed right on Eddie's curly red hair. "Squawk! Birdbrain. Birdbrain."

"Cut that out!" Eddie shook his head and Jack flew to his bird perch.

Melody giggled. "It looks like Jack knows who has a birdbrain."

Howie sat up and rubbed his elbow. "Shhh. Teach must be nearby. We have to get out of here, before it's too late."

The four kids peeked out the door. The trail was clear, so they silently slipped out of the cabin. They were sneaking down the trail when a sound from behind a huge oak stopped them dead in their tracks.

"What might you scallywags be up to? You should be down at the campfire," Teach grumbled in his raspy voice.

The four kids turned to face Teach. Howie shoved the green sunglasses case deeper into his pocket, and Liza squeezed behind Eddie and Melody.

"We're just out exploring the woods," Melody stammered.

"Admiring the plants and stuff," Eddie added.

"Hardee, har, har," laughed Teach. "Then you've found my favorite wild-flower in these woods."

Teach pointed to a group of flowers that were nearly as tall as the kids. "See how those bright orange blossoms hang around the stem like a necklace on a lady's neck?" Teach asked. "They shimmer like gold. Aye, these be my favorite flower in the woods. But they have a secret, too."

"What?" Liza asked.

"Come closer," Teach said. "I'll show you."

The four kids inched closer to Teach as he held up a stem with the dangling orange flowers. "Do you see the green jewel? It hangs beneath the blossom." Teach pointed to a small seed pod. "Go ahead. Touch it."

When Liza reached out and tapped the pod, seeds exploded against her nose.

"Wow! That's neat," Eddie laughed and reached over to tap a few seed pods himself. "An atom bomb flower!"

"What's it called?" Howie asked.

"Some call it jewel-weed," Teach said with a smile. "But others have another name for it. The same thing that Molly the Red said about her very own treasure of riches."

"What?" the four campers asked.

"Touch-me-not!" Teach said. Then he squeezed a dangling pod and sent a seed pinging against Eddie's forehead.

"Squawk! Touch-me-not! Touch-me-not!" Long-Tongued Jack called from the nearby tree.

Teach winked at the campers before him. "Aye, tis best not to touch the jewels of pirates. But the jewel-weed is a jewel of nature, here for us all to enjoy." Then Teach began to laugh. Only this time, his laughter sent cold chills racing up the four kids' backs.

"We'd better get back to camp," Melody said as she backed away from Teach.

"Aye," Teach nodded. "Ye best be trotting back to the others before they think something bad has befallen you."

The four friends left Teach standing next to the clump of jewel-weed and hurried to the campfire. All the other kids were roasting marshmallows and listening to Coach Ellison talk about wildflowers. Howie, Melody, Liza, and Eddie huddled near a huge maple tree.

"Now do you believe Teach is a pirate?" Melody asked Eddie.

Howie nodded. "He's here at Camp Lone Wolf to find Molly the Red's treasure."

"And he knows we have the map. That's why he was warning us against touching the treasure!" Liza whimpered.

Eddie shrugged. "Teach is here to help us win that race against Sheldon. And the only treasure around here is buried in a box of Cracker Jack. He was just showing us a flower in the woods."

Howie shook his head. "I'm not so sure. If the legend about Molly the Red is true, then her treasure is buried on the shores of Red River here at Camp Lone Wolf."

Eddie pointed to the run-down cabins. "If there was a treasure here, Mr. Jenkins would have castles instead of those rat traps."

"Exactly!" Liza blurted. "If we could find that treasure, we could help Mr.

Jenkins save the camp . . . and all these huge old trees."

"There is no treasure," Eddie told her. "And I can prove it."

"How?" Melody asked.

Eddie held out his hand. "Give me the case. I'll prove that Teach is just a boat instructor because I'll prove there's no treasure."

"How can *you* find it if Teach can't?" Howie asked, handing the case to Eddie.

Eddie stuffed the case and map into his back pocket. "Captain Teach doesn't know this place like we do. Besides, he couldn't find it because there isn't a treasure."

"What if Teach figures out you have the map?" Liza asked. "You could be in great danger."

"He won't find out," Eddie bragged. Then he glared at each of his friends.

"Not unless you tell him."

"We won't tell!" they all said together. But none of them noticed the brightly colored bird perched in the tree above them.

7

Molly's Map

"Come on over, kids," Coach Ellison called Melody, Liza, Eddie, and Howie to the campfire. He handed each one a stick with a marshmallow on one end. "There's nothing like marshmallows roasted over an open fire," he told them.

"Unless it's a roasted scoundrel," Captain Teach bellowed as he came up the path.

Eddie gulped and pushed the eyeglasses case deeper into his back pocket before holding his marshmallow above the roaring campfire.

"Nice job this afternoon." Coach Ellison nodded to Teach. "I've never seen a Bailey team row better."

"Tomorrow, we'll see how they fare rowing at a racing speed," Teach said.

"Are you sure their muscles are ready for that?" Coach Ellison asked.

Before Teach could answer, Long-Tongued Jack swooped down from a treetop and flapped around Eddie's head. "Birdbrain! Birdbrain!" he squawked.

"Cut it out!" Eddie yelled and threw a marshmallow at the bird.

All the kids around the campfire laughed. "I think Long-Tongued Jack likes you," Carey teased.

"I'll make that bird into a feather duster if he doesn't leave me alone." Eddie ducked when Long-Tongued Jack soared around him again.

"Molly's Map!" Long-Tongued Jack fluttered over Eddie's head. "Birdbrain! Molly's Map!"

Coach Ellison looked at Teach. "Maybe you'd better call your bird away before someone gets hurt."

Teach looked at Eddie and rubbed his

beard. "Long-Tongued Jack, quit your flapping."

Long-Tongued Jack swooped over Eddie's head and settled on Captain Teach's left shoulder. Teach reached up and gently smoothed Jack's feathers. "There, there. No use getting ruffled on a night as perfect as this."

"Perfect for what?" Carey called out.

Captain Teach held up a telescope and grinned. "The skies are clear and there'll be a full moon this evening. Tis perfect for spying on the stars!"

The campers leaned back and stared into the night sky as Captain Teach pointed to the twinkling dots of light in the darkening sky. "See them shimmer?" he asked. "They sparkle like diamonds in a treasure chest."

"Did you hear that?" Melody hissed.

"Shhh," Howie warned.

"I've spent many a night looking at the sky to help me find my way," Teach continued. Aye, to think that Molly the Red herself gazed upon these very stars!"

"How do you know so much about the sky?" Carey asked.

"Hardee, har, har," Teach laughed. "The stars and the seas are a sailor's friends." He turned and looked straight at Eddie, Melody, Liza, and Howie. His next words made them huddle closer together.

"Haven't you ever heard the old saying? 'Red skies at night, sailors delight. Red skies at morning, sailors take warning.' "

"Squawk!" Long-Tongued Jack added. "Take warning! Take warning!"

8

Sleep

"Did you see the way Teach looked at us?" Melody whispered to Eddie as they walked toward their cabins. It was late, and the tall trees were swaying in the night breeze.

"What do you mean?" Eddie asked.

"Teach knows we have the map," Liza said.

"Shhhh," Eddie sputtered. "Why don't you just announce it to the whole world."

"Long-Tongued Jack already did," Howie said.

"You guys worry too much," Eddie told them. "Tomorrow morning before breakfast we'll have a look around. Then we'll know for sure there isn't any treasure."

"See you tomorrow," Melody said as she and Liza went into the girls' cabin.

Inside the boys' cabin, Eddie tossed and turned all night long. Once, he was sure he heard a wolf howling. Finally, when the first speck of sunlight popped through the dusty window, Eddie slugged Howie in the arm. "Get up," he whispered.

"Leave me alone," Howie mumbled. "It's still dark."

"The sun is shining. Do you want to waste all day sleeping? I thought you wanted to find out about the pirates' treasure."

Howie moaned and pulled the covers over his head. Eddie shook Howie and then looked out the window. In the early morning light he saw a figure moving toward their cabin. The figure had a bird on his shoulder.

"Howie, let's go! Teach is coming for us!" Eddie threw the blankets off his friend.

Howie took a quick peek out the window and gulped. "What do we do?"

"Hurry, grab your clothes! Let's try the back window!" Eddie ran to the back of the cabin and threw open the squeaky window. Sleepy kids from around the room complained about the noise and snuggled deeper into their covers. None of them noticed as Eddie and Howie slipped out the window.

The boys tiptoed away from their cabin and stopped behind the girls' cabin. Then Eddie felt a cold hand on his shoulder.

Eddie tackled the person behind him. It wasn't until they were both on the ground that he noticed the jet-black pigtails.

"Ouch!" Melody hissed. "I think you bruised my arm."

Eddie jumped up and brushed off the seat of his pants. "What are you doing here?" he whispered to Melody.

Melody glared up at Eddie. "We saw Teach heading for the boys' cabin and

thought you might need help. What are you doing here?"

Liza giggled from the shadows of a large hemlock tree. "It looked like they were peeking in the girls' cabin."

Eddie's face turned red. "We were not! We were hiding from Teach."

Howie helped Melody up. "Eddie's right. We'd better get out of here before Teach finds us."

"I'm not scared of that mangy sea mongrel," Eddie snapped.

"You sure sounded scared when you saw him coming to the cabin," Howie said.

"And you jumped like a fish out of water when I touched you," Melody added.

"I don't like surprises," Eddie said. "Except for the kind in a treasure chest. That's what I'm going to hunt for." Eddie marched down the trail leading to the Red River. He didn't bother to look behind him. He knew his three friends would follow.

Eddie stopped on the banks of the river and pulled out the sunglasses case. He was smoothing the wrinkles from the old map when Melody, Liza, and Howie stopped beside him.

"I don't think we were followed," Howie whispered.

Liza shivered. "Teach could come after us at any minute."

Eddie laughed. "He won't have a chance. Coach Ellison will see to it that Teach is rowing down the river with the rest of the kids. That gives us plenty of time to look for this make-believe treasure."

Melody pointed to the map. "It'll be impossible to find the treasure. There's no X to mark the spot."

The treasure hunters silently examined the map for several minutes. Then Liza sighed. "Molly the Red must have liked these beautiful trees, too. She even drew some on her map."

"Only those droopy trees on that little island," Eddie pointed out.

Howie snapped his fingers. "Maybe Molly didn't use an X to show where she hid the treasure."

Eddie rolled his eyes. "All professional pirates used an X."

"Not unless they drew trees instead," Melody said slowly and pointed. "One tree has something written on it."

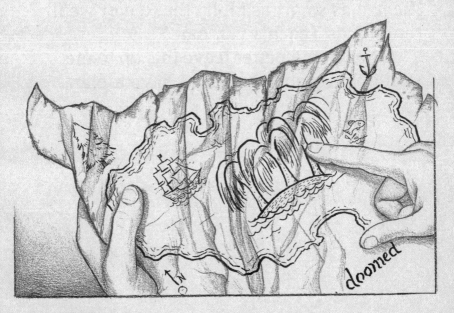

doomed

Liza's eyes got big. "Do you mean Molly buried her treasure under those trees?"

"Exactly," Howie told them.

"What kind of pirate makes their map so hard to figure out?" Eddie snapped.

"A smart one," Melody said.

"Wait, I hear Coach Ellison calling us for breakfast," Howie said.

Liza shivered. "We'd better get back. I don't want Teach to come looking for us."

Howie nodded. "And now we have to be just as smart as Molly the Red or we'll end up as Teach's fish bait."

"Then you'd better leave this up to me," Eddie bragged. "Because I have a plan."

9

Soggy Sneakers

Captain Teach and Coach Ellison kept the kids so busy, Eddie didn't have a chance to put his plan into action. Every morning for three days, the kids practiced rowing. In the afternoon, Coach Ellison took them on a hike, and then in the evening they'd practice rowing again or have a nature lesson. On the fourth day, Eddie decided it was time to try his plan.

Eddie, Melody, Liza, and Howie hid under the dock until all their friends had rowed away from shore. Captain Teach stood on the dock, shouting directions. "Heave to, Bailey Boaters! You'll be needing your muscles today. Faster! Faster!"

Long-Tongued Jack flew from a nearby tree and perched on Teach's shoulder.

Teach straightened the pink sunglasses on his nose and looked into the shadows of the dock. The four hiding kids shrunk further into the shadows. Finally, Teach reached up, smoothed Jack's feathers, and whispered something to the bird. Jack flapped his wings and disappeared into the trees behind the four hiding treasure hunters.

"Can we get out now?" Liza whimpered. "I'm soaking wet."

"We all are," Eddie snapped. "We've been sitting in water for an hour."

Melody patted Liza's shoulder. "Don't be so mean, Eddie. I'm beginning to think your plan is as wet as my sneakers."

"They're out of sight," Howie interrupted. "Let's go."

The kids climbed onto the dock and squeezed water out of their clothes. Eddie left a trail of wet splotches as he jogged to a boat.

"Are you sure this is a good idea?" Melody asked.

"You want to get to that island and look for the treasure, don't you?" Eddie asked.

"But what if we capsize the boat?" Liza cried. "We'll drown!"

Howie shook his head. "We won't as long as we remember everything Teach told us about rowing and we wear life jackets. Besides, Eddie's right. This is our only chance."

"While Teach is busy with the other kids," Melody agreed.

Carefully, the four friends climbed in the boat and strapped on the faded orange life jackets. Howie untied the thick knot that held the boat to the dock, and they each grabbed a set of oars. Without a word they dipped them into the water. The boat silently slid away from the dock.

They were halfway to the small island

when a shadow drifted over the boat. Eddie looked up just in time to see the green feathers diving for his head.

"It's that bird!" he screamed and swatted at Jack with an oar, splashing water all over everyone.

"Stop that!" Liza yelled. "You're getting me wet again."

"Tell that bird to stop," Eddie told her.

Long-Tongued Jack landed on Eddie's head. "Birdbrain! Birdbrain!"

"I'm going to pluck that bird bald!" Eddie slapped at the bird, but Jack flapped away and Eddie ended up hitting himself on the head.

"I hope you knocked some sense into yourself," Melody giggled.

"It's not funny!" Eddie snapped. "But at least I scared that bag of feathers away."

Liza nodded as they reached the shores of the little island. "Maybe he'll leave us alone now."

"These trees aren't little like the ones

on the map," Eddie complained, looking up at the huge towering willows as they pulled the boat onto the island.

"Of course not," Melody told him. "Molly the Red made that map over two hundred years ago. The trees were bound to grow a little since then."

"Look for a tree with something written on it," Liza suggested, "like on the map."

"This is a wild goose chase," Eddie muttered. "Blackbeard probably found the treasure and spent it a long time ago."

"I don't think so," Howie said. "Teach said that Molly's ship sank in 1718. That's the same year Blackbeard died. I bet Molly didn't even know he was dead when she wrote the note."

"Oh, how sad," Liza said.

"But it means the treasure is still here," Melody reminded them. "So start looking."

Eddie held up the map and pointed.

"The tree should be over there if this map isn't a fake."

The kids studied every tree, looking for some clue. All they found was smooth bark and lots of mosquitoes. "I feel like a beaver who can't make up his mind," Eddie complained.

"It's hopeless," Liza agreed, looking at the dozens of trees ahead of them.

"I think this is it!" Melody called. "It looks like something is carved on this tree trunk." Her friends ran over to see.

"Oh, my gosh," Liza yelled. "Molly was really here. This is where she left her treasure!"

Just then a willow tree exploded in a flurry of leaves as Mr. Jenkins pushed through the branches. His beard was full of twigs and leaves, and he looked at them with his red eyes.

"There you are!" Mr. Jenkins growled. "I've been following your trail all morning. Why didn't you stay with the others?"

"We just wanted to see what this island was like," Eddie told him.

Mr. Jenkins looked around and spotted the carvings on the willow tree. He traced over them with his huge hairy hand.

"We didn't do that," Liza blurted. "Honest!"

Mr. Jenkins nodded. "The trees here depend on campers not to carve up their barks. And the rest of the Bailey kids were depending on you to help them in tomorrow's race. They're out there practicing right now! I'd better see you rowing like you've never rowed before!"

The four friends scrambled down the path and leaped into their boat. They were in such a hurry, none of them noticed a big bird flapping down the river toward a distant boat.

10

Sailor Take Warning

"If I learn anything else about trees, I'll sprout roots," Eddie complained. Coach Ellison had just given them a nature lesson on chlorophyll, the green stuff in plants. They were sitting around the campfire after rowing practice.

"I think it's interesting," Howie said. "I like learning about nature."

Eddie shook his head. "I might have known you'd be a green freak. Who needs plants, anyway?"

"You do, nickle brains," Liza told him. "Everything on Earth depends on green plants in some way or another."

"I need green plants like a fly needs bug spray," Eddie told her.

Melody rubbed her arms. "I'm so tired

from rowing, my arms feel like limp tree limbs."

"Like those weeping willow tree branches where the treasure is buried," Liza nodded.

"Yeah, I could use some of that chlorophyll myself," Melody laughed.

"Would you guys stop complaining?" Howie said. "I want to know what we're going to do about the treasure."

"We're going to get it," Eddie said.

Liza stood up and dusted off her shorts. "Don't you remember Teach's warning?" she said.

"I'm not worried about that old hair ball," Eddie bragged. "We'll meet first thing tomorrow and dig up the treasure."

The next morning the kids met behind Cabin Gray Wolf. The sun was just coming up, and the sky was blood-red.

"We'd better not go," Liza whimpered. "Look at that sky."

Howie nodded his head. " 'Red skies at morning, sailors take warning.' "

"We're not sailors," Eddie told them. "We're just kids. But, soon, we're going to be rich like pirates!"

"But we'll miss the race against the Sheldon Sharks," Melody said. "Mr. Jenkins said the team was depending on us."

"What's more important?" Eddie snapped. "A flimsy blue ribbon or a chest full of gold?"

Liza, Melody, and Howie nodded their heads. The four kids silently walked down the trail to the dock. With their life jackets on, they paddled out to the island.

"The treasure's this way," Eddie pointed as they pulled the boat onto shore. He led the way through the trees.

"I bet it's a huge chest filled with diamonds and rubies," Melody giggled.

The four kids stopped in front of the carved tree. "This is it," Howie said.

"It *was* it," Eddie gulped. In front of the tree was a big empty hole.

Melody dropped to her knees and checked the ground. "It's gone all right, but check out these paw prints."

"They look like dog tracks to me," Howie said.

"Or wolf tracks," Liza said. "Don't forget Mr. Jenkins saw us here yesterday."

"That stinky werewolf stole our gold!" Eddie yelled, but he got deathly quiet when he was interrupted by the sharp squawk of a parrot overhead.

11

Dead Heat

"What do you think you're doing?" a deep voice growled from behind them. Liza, Melody, Eddie, and Howie turned around to see Captain Teach waving a stick like a sword. "I knew you were up to no good when I saw you sneaking away from camp."

"Squawk! No good. No good," Long-Tongued Jack added from the drooping branches of a willow tree.

"Your mates were depending on you," Teach said.

The four kids backed against the tree trunk when Teach pointed a dirty finger at Eddie. "What's in your hand?"

Eddie looked down at the crinkled treasure map. He quickly wadded it into a tight ball and tossed it into the hole.

"Nothing," he lied. "Just a piece of paper."

"You scoundrels," Teach growled. Then he lunged forward.

"Run!" Howie screamed.

Long-Tongued Jack swooped down out of the tree and followed the kids as they raced to their boat. "Birdbrain!" he squawked.

"Row like you've never rowed before!" Eddie screamed. They jumped in their boat and paddled like the island was on fire. Not far behind was Teach.

"We'll be okay if we can make it back to Coach Ellison and Mr. Jenkins," Howie yelled as he rowed.

"Great!" Eddie hollered. "Our lives depend on a skinny coach and a werewolf!"

"Be quiet and row!" Melody ordered. The kids concentrated on slapping their oars in the water, but they could still hear Teach gaining on them. In the distance, they saw teams of Bailey Boaters and

Sheldon Sharks gliding through the water.

"Faster, faster!" Howie screamed. The kids rowed with all their might. *Slap, slap.* Their boat pulled away from Teach's. *Slap, slap.* With their muscles aching, they could see the dock at Camp Lone Wolf getting closer and closer.

"I don't think I can make it," Liza cried.

"Don't stop now!" Eddie screamed. "We're almost there!"

Liza, Melody, Howie, and Eddie pulled their oars through the water so fast that they soon passed the other Bailey Boaters and the Sheldon Sharks. Ten strokes later they banged against the dock.

Coach Ellison grabbed their boat and helped them out. "That was the best row-

ing I've ever seen," he congratulated them.

The kids were so out of breath, all they could do was point to Captain Teach in his boat. Coach Ellison nodded his head and grinned. "That Teach is a fantastic rowing instructor."

Then he handed the four boaters blue ribbons. "Let's hear it for the new champions of the annual rowing competition."

The four kids barely heard the cheering crowd. They were too busy staring into the wild eyes of Captain Teach.

12

Progress

Captain Teach took two steps toward the foursome before a group of men and women in business suits pushed him aside. "The race is a fitting end to Camp Lone Wolf," one of the women said as the others nodded.

"What do you mean?" Coach Ellison asked.

"Camp Lone Wolf hasn't paid the bank a red cent for months," a man in a blue suit told him. "We're here to take over this property. This will soon be the site of the biggest mall in the country!"

"But what about the huge old trees?" Howie interrupted.

"And all the wildflowers, like jewelweed and mistletoe!" Liza added. "You can't tear all this down for a mall."

"That's progress," a man in a plaid suit smiled.

"Not to me." The crowd gasped as Mr. Jenkins stepped from the shadows of the forest. His hair was a tangled mess, and deep circles underlined his bloodshot eyes.

"What happened to you?" Coach Ellison asked.

Mr. Jenkins smiled at the crowd. Then his eyes rested on Howie, Melody, Liza, and Eddie. "I've been digging up the money I need to save this place. It looks like the Mega-Mall Development Company will have to look for another place to build."

He faced the men and women in suits. "I treasure this land. Every tree, flower, and animal will always have a home here. Follow me, and we will take care of this matter."

"Wait!" Captain Teach yelled. But as the bankers followed Mr. Jenkins off the

crowded dock, a man in a pinstriped suit accidentally brushed against Teach, pushing him off the dock with a giant splash.

"Squawk! Birdbrain! Birdbrain!" Jack flapped over and landed on Teach's head. Water dripped off his hair, and his glasses hung on one ear.

"I guess we were silly to be afraid of him," Melody laughed, pointing at Captain Teach.

"I wasn't afraid of him," Eddie said, proudly holding his blue ribbon.

"He doesn't look like a pirate, now," Howie said.

"After all," Liza giggled, "who ever heard of a pirate wearing pink sunglasses?"